BALACLAVA BOY

BALACLAVA BOY

by Jenny Robson

illustrations by Sandy Mitchell

Little Island

BALACLAVA BOY

First published in 2009 by Tafelberg, an imprint of NB Publishers, Cape Town, South Africa

This edition published in 2014 by

Little Island Books
7 Kenilworth Park
Dublin 6W
Ireland
www.littleisland.ie

ISBN: 978-1-908195-91-3

A British Library Cataloguing in Publication record for this book is available from the British Library

Cover design adapted from the German-language edition (Tommy Mütze) published by Baobab Books, Basel, Switzerland)

Printed in Poland by Drukarnia Skleniars

Little Island receives financial assistance from The Arts Council (An Chomhairle Ealaíon) and The Arts Council of Northern Ireland

10 9 8 7 6 5 4 3 2 1

In memory of Matt, my best friend

Contents

1

Monday Comprehension

"This sucks!" said Dumisani, my best friend in the world. "This sucks big time!"

"Yeah," I whispered back. "Stupid boring Comprehension!"

There we sat in the front desk in Grade Four SV, not feeling happy. First we had to read this story about some stupid boring boy called Markos. This Markos person was on his way to market. To buy fish or something for his mother. Then there were the Comprehension questions at the end. They were also stupid and boring. Why was Markos walking to market? What did he have in his pocket? Why was he worried?

"Hey, Doogal," Dumisani whispered to me. "I know why this Markos guy is walking."

"Why?"

"Hey, because his Lamborghini's got a flat tyre!"

I laughed. Dumisani is the funniest guy in the world. It's great sitting next to him! Then I thought of something too. "Hey, Dumz. Do you know what's in his pocket?"

"What?"

"His pet baby elephant. Called Spaghetti Nose."

Now Dumisani laughed. "Spaghetti Nose! Good one, Doogz. Okay, so why is he worried?"

I started to answer. "Because . . ."

But then our teacher, Miss Venter, got on our case. "Doogal! Dumisani! Shush!" Miss Venter is always telling us to shush. That's why we have to sit in the front desk. Because we're too talkative. But it's hard to be quiet when you sit next to someone like Dumisani!

Now Cherise stuck her nose in. "Yes, shush, you two! How can I concentrate?"

Cherise sat all by herself in her double desk, right behind us. No one wants to sit next to her. She's very clever and very bossy.

So of course Dumisani and I had to turn round and pull our worst faces at her. But that got Miss Venter, aka the Dragon Lady, on our case again.

"Doogal! Dumisani! Face the front! Dear! Dear! Dear!" Miss Venter is always saying "Dear! Dear! Dear!" Each time

"His pet baby elephant. Called Spaghetti Nose."

she says it, she pats her chest. Then big clouds of white talcum powder rise up from the top of her blouse.

Just then the door opened. In came our headmaster, Mr Rasool, with some new pupil behind him. All of us forgot to stand up. Well, except for Cherise. Mostly, we were in too much shock to be polite. We couldn't believe what we were seeing!

"This is Tommy MacAdam, children," said Mr Rasool, aka Mr Mosi. "Remember, at Colliery Primary we do our best to make new pupils feel welcome. So be kind and thoughtful."

And we all forgot to say "Yes, Sir". Even Cherise. We were too busy staring at this new guy, Tommy. He was wearing an ordinary green Colliery Primary tracksuit. He had ordinary brown eyes. But that was all that was ordinary about him. The rest of his face – his nose, his mouth, his cheeks, even his hair – was hidden under a balaclava! A red-and-orange striped balaclava! How about that?!

The poor new boy had to sit next to Cherise. That was the only empty seat. Miss Venter gave him a book so he could do the Comprehension too. Cherise kept bossing him around and explaining on and on about Markos and his fish.

But Dumisani and I had stopped caring about this

"This is Tommy MacAdam, children."

"Hey, Doogz, maybe he's got a big red birthmark on his cheek."

6

Markos and his stupid boring shopping. We had more interesting stuff to think about. Like: Why, why, why was the new guy wearing a balaclava?

"This is weird, Doogz," Dumisani whispered.

"It's – it's bizarre," I whispered back. My big sister is always calling stuff 'bizarre'. I don't know exactly what it means. But it sounded just right.

"Hey, Doogz, maybe he's got a big red birthmark on his cheek. You know, like Transformer in Grade Seven."

"Or maybe," I whispered back, "maybe he was in a fire and his face got burned. Or he was in an accident so he's got scars all over. Like Mr Davids in Aloe Street."

But Miss Venter, aka the Dragon Lady, was on our case again.

"Doogal! Dumisani! Dear! Dear! Dear!" Pat pat pat went her hand on her chest. Puff puff puff: three clouds of Lily of the Valley powder covered her face. It's the same powder my mom uses sometimes. I know the smell well.

Still Dumisani held up his Comprehension book so he could whisper behind it. "Break-time, Doogz. He'll have to take the thing off to eat his lunch, right? Then we'll get to see what's underneath."

After all, Mr Rasool said we must be kind.

2

Monday Break-Time

We walked around the playground with the new boy, one on each side. After all, Mr Rasool said we must be kind.

"My name's Dumisani," said Dumisani. "And this guy's Doogal. Or you can call us the Doo Dudes. That's our aka."

Tommy nodded his balaclava.

Then we started asking him question after question. Where did you live before? What school did you go to? Is your dad at the Coal Mine or the Power Station? Most of our dads work at the Coal Mine or the Power Station. Some of our moms too. Way off over the roof tops, you can see the huge cooling towers puffing steam into the air. Sometimes you can hear the steam engines carrying coal from the Mine.

Do you have brothers and sisters? Do you have a Play Station?

I wanted to laugh. We sounded just like a stupid boring Comprehension ourselves! The only question we didn't ask was: Why are you wearing that thing on your head?

Tommy answered all the questions through his red-and-orange stripes. It was quite hard to hear what he was saying. At last he sat down and opened his lunch-box. Dumisani and I sat down too, one on each side of him. We held our breath.

But we held our breath for nothing! Tommy didn't take off his balaclava. He just pulled the stripes away from his neck and his mouth and slid his tomato sandwich up underneath. It was very disappointing.

Our friend Obakeng was yelling at us now. "Hey, Doo Dudes. Let's have ourselves some soccer! Bring that new guy along."

Tommy was a bit nervous at first. "Me too? Are you sure? I only ever played a few times before. So I'm not sure . . ."

But Dumisani promised he'd help and explain stuff. And then we ran down to the field. X-man and Riyaad and Johan Eksteen Clayton and Moketsi from our class were there already. Plus some guys from Grade Four JH.

Tommy turned out to be one mean player. Very mean!

Especially for someone with most of his head covered.

When the bell rang, Obakeng, aka Ostrich Legz, yelled, "Hey, Balaclava Boy! Tomorrow you're on my side. Okay, bru?"

"You shouldn't be so nosey!" Cherise was bossing us around from the girls' line. "It's Tommy's private business. If Mr Rasool says he's allowed to wear it, then it's got nothing to do with you two."

"You shouldn't be so nosey!"

We were lined up on the netball court with the rest of the school. Obakeng yanked Tommy into the front of the boys' line with him. But Dumisani and I got stuck half-way down, close to Cherise. She was giving us a lecture as usual.

. . . Stupid boring Geography.

"You wait!" Dumisani told her. "Straight after school, soon as we're out the gates, we're going to ask him. Straight out. When there's no one else around. Then first thing to-morrow we'll tell you why!"

"Yeah," I added. "Because you're dying to know, Cherise. Come on, don't pretend. You and everyone else."

And it was the truth! All the rest of the Grade Fours were staring at our new boy. Plus the Grade Five NM bullies. Even the Grade Six snobs were having a good look.

Miss Venter waited to lead us back to class for stupid boring Geography. Well, it was stupid and boring at the moment. Who cares where maize gets grown? Who cares when apples get ripe?

"First thing tomorrow, Cherise," Dumisani was promising. "You just wait . . ."

But Miss Venter was on our case again. "Dumisani! Doogal! Cherise! Dear! Dear! Dear!"

3

Tuesday Maths

"So, Double Trouble? Did you find out?" Cherise wanted to know, first thing on Tuesday morning.

It was early, long before line-up. The Power Station siren was only just going off. Thandi and Hannah were only just starting their clapping game, chanting at the tops of their voices. Thandi and Hannah do everything at the tops of their voices!

It was weird, being at school early. Usually I have to wait and wait outside Dumisani's house. Usually he comes rushing out, still eating his toast. And with his bag and his tracksuit half-zipped. And then we have to run like mad to get to school before the line-up bell. This morning, instead, he was the one waiting for me!

"And so, Double Trouble? What's the answer then?"

Thandi and Hannah do everything at the tops of their voices!

Cherise was there on the netball court with her hands on her hips.

Dumisani and I hate being called Double Trouble. Our proper nickname is the Doo Dudes. Or else, the Big Ds. Even though only Dumisani is big. I'm quite small. Nearly as small as Yasmiena.

So we put down our bags and pretended Cherise wasn't even there.

"That's strange, Doogz," Dumisani said. "I thought Cherise said we shouldn't be nosey."

"Yeah, you're right, Dumz," I said. "I'm sure she said it was Balaclava Boy's private business."

Cherise was getting annoyed now. "Grow up!" she told us. Cherise is always telling Grade Fours to grow up. Especially us.

Dumisani seemed like he was going to tease Cherise some more. But then he changed his mind. "Okay, Cherise. We asked Tommy. Straight out, right? And he said, 'Because.' That's all."

"Because?" Cherise frowned hard under her fringe.

We nodded. That was the truth. That's the only answer Tommy gave us there outside the school gates.

Cherise put her hands on her hips again. "That's not a proper answer! It has to be 'Because – something.' You can't say 'Because' and then stop. That doesn't make sense!"

Just then, Tommy walked through the school gates. Today he was wearing a navy blue balaclava.

For a second, I wanted to run over and yank that navy blue balaclava right off his head and see what was underneath. But of course you can't do stuff like that. No matter how much you want to. It's rude. It's mean.

Cherise said, "You watch, Big Ds. I'll get a proper answer. I'll use psychology."

'Psychology'! That sounded like a good word! I said it over in my mind a few times to remember it.

But Dumisani laughed. "Bet you it doesn't work, Clever Clogs." Then we ran down to join the early morning soccer game. Tommy was already there, playing on Obakeng's side. He even scored a goal! We had a great time. Well, until the Grade Five NM bullies stole our ball. The Grade Five NM bullies are always doing stuff like that.

But the line-up bell was going anyway.

All through stupid boring Maths and stupid boring decimal fractions, Dumisani and I kept quiet. We were waiting to hear Cherise start her psychology. The other Grade Fours were surprised, I think. They aren't used to us two working in silence.

First Obakeng, aka Ostrich Legz, pretended he needed

to sharpen his pencil. On his way to the bin, he whispered, "Hey, Doo Dudes. What's wrong, my bruz? Are you guys sick or something?"

Then Johan Eksteen Clayton, aka JECO, pretended he needed to borrow Riyaad's ruler. He also whispered as he passed our desk. "Eish! Are you okay, Big Ds?" That's his favourite word: 'eish!' He uses it every time he speaks. No matter what else he's saying!

And then Thandi, who is very noisy anyway, blew her nose extra-loud. She went to throw her tissue away, then bent over our desk. "Wazzup, Dumisani? Wazzup, Doo-

gal? Have you taken a vow of silence?"

Miss Venter was getting annoyed. She told them to stop behaving like jack-in-the-boxes. Then she told Dumisani and me that she was very pleased with us for working so quietly.

And then she told Billy de Beer, aka Lost In Space, to stop staring out the window. Billy de Beer spends all his time staring out of windows. That's why he's called Lost In

Billy de Beer spends all his time staring out of windows.

Space.

Finally, finally, Cherise got going. We were already doing sum number 5.

"Tommy," we heard her say. So we leaned back to hear better. "Tommy, do you know why we call Miss Venter the Dragon Lady?"

"Nah. Why?" Tommy said through his balaclava.

"Because," said Cherise.

"What do you mean, 'Because'?" said Tommy. "Because why?"

"Oh, do you mean you want a reason?" We could hear in Cherise's voice that she was smiling. "Okay, well, I'll give you a reason. It's because Miss Venter pats her chest and then her powder comes puffing out. And last year we learned a song called 'Puff the Magic Dragon'. So that's why."

Dumisani and I looked at each other and shook our heads. This psychology stuff took one long, long time to start working!

"Okay, Tommy. Now I'm going to ask you a question. And you have to give me a reason too."

Dumisani and I held our breath.

But Miss Venter was on Cherise's case. "Is that you talking? Again? What's got into you this week, my girl? Dear! Dear! Dear!"

"Because," said Cherise.

*"Okay, Tommy. Now I'm going to ask you a question.
And you have to give me a reason too."*

That kept Cherise quiet for the rest of the lesson. She hates getting into trouble with teachers! We didn't hear another sound from her until stupid boring Maths was over and stupid boring Natural Science started. Well, it was stupid and boring at the moment. Who cares what fishes' fins get called? Why can't we rather do great white sharks? Or tsunamis?

4

Tuesday Natural Science

Dumisani was busy drawing a cowboy hat and dreadlocks on his fish. I was busy labelling my dorsal fin. Miss Venter was safe across the classroom, trying to help Billy de Beer, aka Lost In Space, to concentrate.

That's when Cherise got going again. "Okay, Tommy," she whispered. "Now I want you to tell me why you're wearing a balaclava."

But Tommy gave her the same answer he'd given us. "Because."

"Because – why?" Cherise demanded in her bossiest voice.

"Because – because," Tommy said. And then he kept silent. No matter how much Cherise bossed him around. Or talked on and on about reasons and explanations.

Dumisani and I went back to our fishes. Dumisani labelled his gills. I gave my fish an iPod and some spectacles so he looked a bit like Moketsi. But Cherise hadn't given up. She never gives up easily.

Miss Venter was busy looking for something in the back cupboard now. So Cherise whispered, "Tommy, do you know what we call Mr Rasool?"

"The headmaster? Nah, what?"

"We call him Mr Mosi. Do you know why?"

"Nah. Why?"

"Because."

But Tommy knew what she was trying to do this time. So he just said, "Ha ha, very funny!"

And of course Dumisani and I had to turn round and say, "Ha ha, Cherise. Very funny," as well. And then the bell rang and it was the end of gills and scales and dorsal fins.

"See, Smartie Pants," Dumisani teased Cherise. "Your psychology stuff is useless! But don't worry! The Doo Dudes are moving on to Plan B."

"Yeah," I agreed, even though I didn't know what Plan B was yet. "You just watch and learn!"

Cherise walked off with Mpho, aka Mousie Mousie, telling her that we were the most childish, irritating boys in Grade Four SV. Mpho said nothing. Mpho never says anything. Not ever.

When home-time came, we swung into action with Dumisani's Plan B. It was a stunning plan. The best! We followed Tommy at a distance all the way to his home on Daffodil Street. We acted like proper secret service spies, hiding behind hedges and parked cars so Tommy wouldn't spot us.

Once he was in his house, we crept around the side. There were some wooden crates there. So we stacked them against the wall and climbed up on them. Then we were tall enough to see through the window.

Tommy was already in the room. His mom came in and gave him a big hug. She said, "How was school, sweet-

We acted like proper secret service spies.

Tommy lifted up both hands and began to pull off his balaclava.

heart? Did you find someone nice to be friends with? This is the last time we're going to move, promise. Dad's taken a permanent job here now."

Then Tommy lifted up both hands and began to pull off his balaclava. Dumisani and I held our breath. Again.

5

Wednesday Questions

"And then? What happened then?" Cherise wanted to know. First thing on Wednesday morning. Dumisani and I were at school early again. Long before line-up. For the second day in a row!

"Come on, Doo Dudes, tell me!" Cherise had her hands on her hips. But at least she was calling us by our proper nickname.

So we told her the rest of our spy story. It didn't have a good ending. Dumisani's wooden crate had broken under him with a loud crack. Then a huge dog, a Rottweiler or something, came rushing and snarling round the corner. With huge strings of saliva dangling and swinging from its vampire teeth.

"We had to run for our lives!" Dumisani said. "It would

have ripped us apart! So we didn't see Tommy with his bala-clava off."

Cherise shook her head at us like we were total idiots.

"But don't worry," I said, "because now we're going to try Plan C." I'd only just thought of Plan C, right at that moment! I whispered it to Dumisani so Cherise couldn't hear.

With huge strings of saliva dangling and swinging from its vampire teeth.

Dumisani laughed. "Hey, Doogz! That's not a bad idea! Let's hit the road!"

So we rushed around the playground, explaining Plan C to everyone in Grade Four SV. Except Cherise, of course. Down at the soccer field, we told Obakeng and Riyaad and the rest. We made Thandi and Hannah stop their clapping game long enough to listen.

We found Donna-Kyle, aka Factfile, aka Discovery Channel. She was under a tree with an encyclopaedia and Mpho, aka Mousie Mousie.

Donna-Kyle nodded. "That might work, Big Ds. I must admit, I'm getting really curious."

Mpho said nothing. As usual.

And then Tommy arrived with his school bag and a beige balaclava with white stripes.

My Plan C was going like a Boeing. Purring like a Porsche! Racing like a Lamborghini in fifth gear!

We sat in class, writing notes about cleaning your teeth. But everyone had more important stuff to think about than dental floss.

Mostly, everyone was trying to find an excuse to walk past Tommy's desk.

Hannah managed first.

She stuck up her hand and her voice boomed out:

"Please, Miss. Can I get my pink pencil crayon, Miss? From Beatrice, Miss. For the gums on the diagram, Miss."

She walked to Beatrice's desk the long way round. As she passed Tommy, she bent and whispered through his balaclava: "Hey, dude, why are you wearing that thing?"

"Hey, dude, why are you wearing that thing?"

"I'm desperate, Miss," he groaned.

Then Obakeng put up his long, long arm so his tracksuit sleeve slid down to his elbow. "Please, Miss, I need the toilet."

"Is it urgent, Obakeng?"

Obakeng screwed up his face like he was suffering big time. "I'm desperate, Miss," he groaned. But he wasn't so desperate that he didn't have time to stop at Tommy's desk.

"Hey, New Bru," he whispered. "We really need to know. Why have you got that thing on your head?"

And so it went on.

And on.

Dumisani and I smiled while we drew caps and scarves and smiley faces on our tooth diagrams. So they looked like rows of soccer fans.

We were sure: sooner or later Tommy would get sick of hearing the same question.

Sooner or later he'd crack. He'd tell us what we were all dying to know. Just to make us stop!

Even Billy, aka Lost In Space, found an excuse to walk past Tommy's desk. Once he got there, he forgot what he was supposed to say. But at least he tried.

Miss Venter was losing her patience, though. "What's got into all of you? You're like jack-in-the-boxes! Worse than yesterday. Dear! Dear! Dear!"

Thandi started coughing. Loudly, of course.

She patted her chest until powder hung like a cloud over our heads. Thandi started coughing. Loudly, of course.

But Tommy, aka Balaclava Boy, aka New Bru, didn't crack. No matter how many Grade Fours leaned over his desk. The only answer he whispered back was "Because". After a while, he stopped even saying that much.

6

Wednesday Answers

Dumisani and I knelt down by our bags to get our lunch-boxes. We weren't feeling happy. And Cherise just made it worse.

She smirked down at us. She said, "If you want something done properly, then you have to get a girl to sort it. Now you two can watch and learn!"

She spent the whole break whispering to the other Grade Fours while they skipped or ate their lunch or played soccer. Or went to the duty teacher, Mrs Twetwe, to complain that the Grade Fives had stolen their ball. Again.

We followed Cherise around the playground. But the only thing we heard her say was, "Don't tell Tommy. And don't tell the Doo Dudes. It's a surprise."

And no one would tell us either. Not Obakeng nor

X-man nor Riyaad, aka Rough Stuff.

After break, things got weird. It was creative writing. We were supposed to write a story about 'My Most Exciting Holiday' for Miss Venter. But instead, everyone else was scribbling on pieces of paper. And then they passed their notes along the rows to Cherise. Carefully, so Miss Venter

Everyone else was scribbling on pieces of paper.

didn't notice.

We kept turning around, Dumisani and I. But Cherise kept slipping the notes into her dictionary. Quickly, so we couldn't see. She was smirking again. And her dictionary

got fatter and fatter.

"This sucks!" said Dumisani. "This sucks big time!"

We gave up. We went back to writing about our stupid boring Most Exciting Holidays.

By the time the home-bell rang, we were going crazy with curiosity.

We didn't rush out the classroom with the others. Instead we hung around Cherise's desk, hoping.

In the end she made us go down on our knees. Right down on both knees – well, all four knees – and beg.

We had to promise never to be rude to her again. Nor

We had to say that yes, girls were much cleverer than boys.

pull faces at her.

We had to say that yes, girls were much cleverer than boys.

It was embarrassing! But at least there was no one else left in the classroom to see. It was just us three. Well, us three plus the head cleaner, Mr Plaatjies, aka Rocket Man, aka Cape Canaveral. He was sweeping at full throttle, making the dust fly with his supersonic broom.

"Okay," Cherise said at last. She opened up her dictionary. "There you go."

The notes were awesome! Stunning! Completely worth begging for! They were all the reasons why our classmates thought Tommy wore a balaclava. We read them one by one.

Cos his ears are big and they stik out like cabiges so he gets imbarissed. Love from Hannah.

Because all his hairs fell out. From Moketsi aka THE TERMINATOR.

His Mommy said he must because it is winter. Leila January.

Coz hez a famous football star and hez hiding from all his fanz. BY: Xavier Fernandez aka X-man.

Dumisani and I read on and on. And on. We forgot all about it being home-time. And Cherise didn't rush us. She

She just kept putting more notes in front of us.

just kept putting more notes in front of us.

His mother loves knitting but she can only knit bala-clavas cos she only got a pattern for balaclavas so she can't knit other things. Love Yasmiena.

Eish! Cos he is so ugly. He will make us scared if we ever see his face. Maybe we will turn into rock from shock. Eish! Even uglier than Gary penfold in grade Seven. By Johan Eksteen Clayton.

Becos he doesn't want to get germs like sars and mad cow DISEES so it works like a mask or otherwise maybe he has got a DISEES so he doesn't want us to catch it. Written by Riyaad Desai aka Rough Stuff aka WWF aka THE STRONGEST BOY IN THE SCHOOL.

There was an extra-long, extra-amazing one by Mpho, aka Mousie Mousie. She wrote that Tommy might be in a witness protection programme because he'd seen a murder. And the police had told Mr Rasool that Tommy must keep his face covered. In case the murderer's friends tried to silence him.

"I wonder why she keeps so quiet when she can think of stuff like this?!" Dumisani said.

Then there was a weird reason from Obakeng in his weird writing that was as long and skinny as his arms and legs.

Its coz the New Bru is n ALIEN. With a purple nose n green lips. He got sent to Earth 2 C how intlgnt we R. Shame he must sit bhind the Big Dz. Coz now he thinx we R all IDIYOTS. – Only joking, Dumz + Doogz. From Obakeng aka O-Rang-O-Tang Armz.

Even Billy de Beer had written something. It wasn't anything to do with Tommy or the balaclava. Instead it was about some weaverbird's nest in the tree outside. But at least he tried.

"See, this is my plan," Cherise explained. "On Friday I'm going to read them all out for Free Orals. Then maybe Tommy will get sick of hearing the wrong reasons. So he'll maybe tell us the right one." She packed the notes back in her dictionary and put her dictionary in her case.

Dumisani and I ran home together. Fast, in case his mom was worrying.

"Do you reckon Cherise's plan will work?" I asked when I got some breath.

But Dumisani didn't answer. He just ran on with his bag bouncing against his back. I knew what his problem was. He was worried that Cherise would use up all the Free Orals time with her notes. And then he wouldn't get a chance.

Dumisani loves doing Friday Free Orals. It's his favourite lesson of the whole week. He loves standing up in front of everyone, talking on and on. And on! Without Miss Venter or anyone telling him to shush.

7

Thursday Assembly

But on Thursday we forgot all about Cherise's plan for Free Orals. Thursday was the day of The Attack. For a long time afterwards, Grade Four SV talked about that day.

Like every Thursday, it started with Assembly. All of us from Grade One to Grade Seven sat on the hall floor. In our green tracksuits. We looked like one huge bumpy sloping indoor lawn. Tommy was wearing his red-and-orange striped balaclava again. So it looked like some confused bird had dropped an apricot on the grass.

Our headmaster, Mr Rasool, aka Mr Mosi, was talking about being kind. Most times in Assembly he talks about being kind. Or caring for others.

"Children," he said. "There is so much cruelty in this world! We must not add to it. No! We must be sunbeams of joy and kindness."

Mr Rasool had tears in his eyes. He often gets tears in his eyes when he speaks about stuff like kindness. Sometimes the tears run down his cheeks.

But the Grade Five NM bullies didn't want to be sunbeams of joy and kindness! No! They sat just behind Balaclava Boy. And Dumisani and I could hear the mean things they were whispering.

"Hey, Sock-head! Are you hiding a pumpkin in there? Or maybe you've got a squashed tomato for a head?"

Are you hiding a pumpkin in there?

"Hey, Tea-cosy-brain! What happens when you sneeze? Yuck! Snot squashed everywhere!"

We Doo Dudes shifted up closer to Tommy. In case he was feeling bad about being new and being mocked.

After Assembly there was a stupid boring spelling test. Cherise got twenty out of twenty. As usual. She bounced around her desk like this was the first time she'd ever got full marks. Poor Tommy! He nearly went sliding right off onto the floor.

Then Miss Venter put us in groups to do a transport worksheet about steam engines. That was more fun. In my group, I had a huge argument with Sheldon about which one was faster: a Ferrari or a Maserati. Well, until our group leader, Yasmiena, got upset.

"Doogal! Sheldon! Shush!" she ordered. "We've got to draw a steam engine now. So quit jabbering about other stuff!" Yasmiena is quite bossy. Even if she is so tiny that her plaits nearly reach the ground.

Dumisani's group sat on the carpet behind me. So I could hear him having a huge argument with Donna-Kyle. About their drawing.

"I'm telling you, Big D," Donna-Kyle was saying, "you can't draw a train-surfer on top of a steam train. They didn't have train-surfers in the old days. So rub him out!"

"Aah, come on, man! Live a little," Dumisani argued back. "I bet Billy likes my train-surfer. Don't you, Billy?" But of course Billy was too busy looking out the window to answer.

Yes, it was good fun! Best of all, Miss Venter didn't tell us to shush. We were supposed to be talking, discussing the worksheet. So the Dragon Lady just walked around the classroom smiling.

And then came break. And The Attack.

Dumz and I were just finishing off his banana yoghurt when we saw something really bad. The Grade Five NM bullies were dragging Tommy off to the bush behind Mr Plaatjies' shed.

Everyone knows the kind of stuff that goes on behind that shed!

We jumped up. We rushed to the soccer field to scream for Riyaad and JECO and the rest.

"Tommy's in trouble! The bullies have got Balaclava Boy! Let's go! Let's move it!"

By the time we reached the bush behind the shed, the situation was drastic. The bullies had Tommy down on the gravel. They were holding his legs to stop him kicking. They were punching his arms to make him let go of his balaclava.

Tommy's in trouble!

Tommy held on as tightly as he could. But he was losing the battle. Already his neck was showing. And part of his chin. There was a bright red stain on the wool above his nose. It looked more like blood than a red stripe.

He was screeching louder than the Power Station siren. "Leave me alone! Ow! O-O-O-O-W!"

We rushed in to rescue him. We used all the strength we had. Riyaad, aka Rough Stuff, aka WWF, was head-butting their leader, Cedric Carson, in the stomach. Obakeng whirled his long arms round and round like helicopter blades. Dumisani and I knelt there next to Tommy's head, trying to yank Grade Five fingers off his balaclava. And Moketsi yelled at the top of his voice, "I'll tell Miss Venter! I'll tell Mr Rasool! You wait! You'll all get expelled!"

It was hopeless, though. We didn't really stand a chance, not even with Riyaad on our side. The bullies were bigger and stronger and much, much meaner. Already part of Tommy's bottom lip was showing under the bloodstain.

Just then Cherise appeared with Mrs Twetwe, the teacher on duty.

Mrs Twetwe is mega-large and mega-strict and big time fierce and scary! She's the only teacher in the whole school without a nickname. No one has ever dared to think up one for her. Not even the Grade Sevens.

Mrs Twetwe blew her duty whistle. Hard! Everyone stopped to cover their poor ears. "The whole lot of you: Mr Rasool's office! Now!" she commanded. No one dared to argue.

8

Thursday Sixth Period

"Fighting?!" Mr Rasool shook his head sadly at all of us. "Children, our world is full of violence. And now you want to add more? Right here in Colliery Primary?"

Big tears started running down our headmaster's cheeks. They plopped onto the papers on his desk. But then he noticed the blood staining Tommy's balaclava. So he sent us Grade Fours back to Miss Venter. The Grade Fives had to stay behind and listen some more.

Dumisani and I walked with Tommy safe between us. Tommy was limping and rubbing his arm. But he didn't seem bothered. Instead he wanted to talk about Mr Rasool.

"I just can't believe it!" Balaclava Boy said. "I've been to seven different schools. Seven! Even a school overseas in Scotland. But I've never, ever seen a headmaster cry before. Nor even a headmistress."

"That's why we call him Mr Mosi," said Dumisani.

"Why Mr Mosi?"

"Well, New Bru," Dumisani explained, "it's short for Mosi-oa-Tunya. You know, the other name for Victoria Falls."

Tommy nodded his red-and-orange striped head. "I get it!" he laughed. I was happy to see he could still laugh. He was being really brave.

Back in class Miss Venter told us to get out our stupid boring reading books. Even though it was sixth period and not reading time. Then she took Tommy off to our first-aid lady, Mrs Modise, aka the Germolene Queen.

"Keep reading until we get back," Miss Venter said at the door.

But even Cherise couldn't concentrate on her reading. She kept tapping her pencil on her desk like she was squashing ants. Then she went to stand in front.

"Listen, class," she said. She sounded like Miss Venter. "For Free Orals tomorrow, I'm not going to read out your notes. Is that okay? I know you worked hard on them. But I think we must leave Tommy in peace about his balaclava and stop bugging him. He's had enough hassles. We don't

"Listen, class," she said.

want him to feel worse. He can tell us when he's ready to tell us. So is that okay?"

Up and down the rows, everyone agreed.

"Cool."

"No problem."

"Fine by me."

"Yeah, poor guy! Give him a break!"

And that was the moment Dumisani and I suddenly looked at each other. We just knew we were both thinking the same thing. We both had exactly the same idea. It happens with us sometimes. I suppose because we've been friends since we were little.

"Hey, Cherise," I said. "This is just an idea, right? But what about . . . ? Nah!" I stopped. Maybe our idea would sound silly.

"What about what, Doogal?" Cherise was still in front, still sounding like a teacher.

"Well, why don't we ask everyone . . . ? Nah. They'd never do it."

Cherise was getting impatient. "Never do what, Doogal?"

Dumisani took over now. "Nah, you'll probably just think it's stupid."

Cherise put her hands on her hips. "Oh, grow up, Big Ds. Just tell me."

We both had exactly the same idea.

So we did. Well, Dumisani did. He stood up in the front too and explained.

And we were in for a surprise! Cherise thought it was a brilliant idea! Absolutely brilliant! So did everyone else! They clapped and cheered. Obakeng gave one of his whistles – long and ear-splitting. Thandi and Hannah and Innocent yelled, "Party-time! Party-time!" at the tops of their voices.

*So of course Dumisani and I had to stand up
on our desk and bow to all our fans.*

So of course Dumisani and I had to stand up on our desk and bow to all our fans.

The noise went on and on until Miss Venter and Tommy got back from the Germolene Queen. With Tommy smelling of Savlon.

After school, Dumz and I escorted Tommy all the way home to Daffodil Street. We strode with our backs straight and our arms swinging wide. We did our best to look mean and scary. We scanned the whole area for danger. Most of all, we kept silent. Like proper secret service bodyguards.

Well, until we got to Tommy's gate. Then Dumisani said, "You wait! There's a surprise for you tomorrow!"

"What surprise?" asked Balaclava Boy. But then his mom appeared and saw the bloodstain and got very upset.

Dumz and I walked on towards Frangipani Road. That's where we both live. Where we've always lived. Nearly opposite each other.

We passed a small red house on a corner. And we stopped. It used to be the house of our Grade Two teacher, Mrs Godfrey.

Mrs Godfrey had got very sick. And around the playground, a terrible word was whispered: 'Cancer'. After that we only saw Mrs Godfrey a few times, sitting on her verandah or in her husband's car. She always wore a head-scarf.

And another word was being whispered around the playground: 'Chemotherapy'. Especially by the Grade Sevens. Chemotherapy was special hospital treatment for cancer. It made all your hair fall out.

Dumisani and I stood outside the small red house with its empty verandah.

"You don't think . . . ?" I said. "What if maybe Tommy . . . ?" It was such an awful thought. Too awful to say out loud.

But after a while Dumisani shook his head. "Nah, Doogz. Because look how he runs around the soccer field. Like a mad thing! Look at the way he sends that ball flying. He couldn't do that if he was sick, could he?"

So we headed on to Frangipani Road. Walking quickly towards the sound of steam trains shunting as they carried coal from the Mine to the Power Station.

There was lots to do. We had to sort out stuff for tomorrow's Brilliant Idea. And I had to make up something to say for Free Orals. In case Miss Venter chose me.

Dumisani never prepares anything, though. He just stands up in front and the words come tumbling out of his mouth. He's so good, he can get the class yelling stuff back at him. Miss Venter calls that 'Audience Participation'. Du-misani's Free Orals always have lots of Audience Partici-pation. And they're always great fun.

9

Friday Surprise

On Friday, Tommy wore his navy balaclava again. We hardly noticed. There was too much else to stare at. Our whole classroom had turned into one very strange, very bizarre place!

Miss Venter looked around with her eyes wide. She kept shaking her head very slowly, not saying a word. Not even "Dear! Dear! Dear!" The whole class – all of us – were wearing balaclavas of some kind! Every single one of us in Grade Four SV!

Me – I'd borrowed my granny's tea-cosy. It was a pink-and-purple crocheted one with three pink-and-purple flowers on the top. I had a problem with seeing, though. The hole for the tea-pot handle was long and narrow. So I could only look with one eye at a time.

And Dumisani had his cousin's army balaclava on. It was very smart, made of camouflage material. It was also much too big. Dumisani kept yanking it around, but there were still bunches of extra material everywhere.

"Isn't this awesome, Doogz?" Dumisani said through his bunches.

I nodded hard so my three flowers bounced around on top of my head. "It's – it's surreal," I answered. 'Surreal' is also one of my big sister's favourite words.

We turned round to check if Tommy was enjoying his surprise. He was definitely smiling. We knew by the way his eyes crinkled up.

I left my stupid boring decimal fractions and went to the bin to sharpen my pencil. Mostly so I could have a better look. And it was a mega-awesome, mega-surreal sight! Even with only one eye! Thirty-one covered heads bobbed above the desks. Like round balloons!

Obakeng was wearing an old black beanie. He'd pulled it down to his chin. And he'd cut a very skew, very jagged hole to see through. X-man and Riyaad and Innocent, aka Guilty, all wore pantyhose legs. Their foreheads and noses were squashed flat. They looked fierce and quite crazy.

Then there was Johan Eksteen Clayton. He had a towel or something wrapped round his head, held together with nappy pins. His eye-hole was even more jagged than Obakeng's. Bits of towel-fluff lay all over his tracksuit top. Like he'd been in a snowstorm. He kept trying to brush it off, saying "Eish! Eish!" under his breath.

Cherise wore a bright pink ski mask. It belonged to her mom's friend, who went skiing on some snowy mountains called the Alps. That's what she told us. Two bright pink pompoms dangled from her head like furry ears. Even Billy de Beer, aka Lost In Space, had a scarf tied round his nose and mouth. Like a Wild West gunfighter.

"Who on earth is that at the bin?!" Miss Venter was speaking again after the shock wore off a bit. "Tyrone? Melissa? Mariam? Doogal? Whoever you are, I'm sure your pencil is sharp by now. Sit down and get on with your sums! Dear! Dear! Dear!"

Break-time was even more fun. All us soccer guys went rushing past the benches where the Grade Five bullies sat. Shouting insults at them through our balaclavas. Everything we could think of.

"Hey, you bunch of losers!"

"Hey, you brain-dead, knobbly-knee idiots!"

"Hey, Babies. Did you get lost on your way to Tele-tubby Crèche? It's that way, Babies."

For today we were safe. The bullies couldn't tell who

"Hey, you bunch of losers!"

was who. They mostly stared at us, looking confused. Or maybe Mr Rasool's lecture was still on their minds.

"Isn't this great, being incognito?" Donna-Kyle said to us. She was under her white balaclava, under her tree with her encyclopaedia on her lap. "I could be a famous film star. Or a Nobel scientist. My dad could be a cabinet minister. Or the Mine manager. I could pretend to be anyone."

Tommy gave a star performance

That was a nice-sounding word: 'incognito'. I said it over in my mind to remember it. And then we rushed down to the soccer field. It was a bit hopeless, though. No one could work out who was in whose team. So we mostly ran around kicking the ball in all directions and scoring goals any time we got near the nets.

Tommy gave a star performance. He took the ball all the way from midfield to the penalty box. Even Lucky, aka AC Milan, couldn't rob him. Well, if it was Lucky inside the green pantyhose leg with the shiny butterfly sequins!

Library was straight after break. Mr Abrahamse nearly had a heart attack when we led in.

"What is this now? How must I teach mind maps to students I don't even recognise? Maybe I'm stuck in some bank robbery no one's bothered to mention to me? Or a hijacking? I don't even own a car and here I am, surrounded by a gang of hijackers!"

Mr Abrahamse, aka Did You Wash Your Hands?, went to complain to the headmaster.

But Mr Rasool didn't scold us. He stood in front of the library posters with tears in his eyes. "I understand, children. You are trying to be kind and welcoming to Tommy. Am I right? Behaving just the way Colliery Primary children should behave."

So Mr Abrahamse went on teaching stupid boring mind maps to students he couldn't see. Until the bell rang and it was time for Free Orals.

We lined up to lead back to class. Dumisani's eyes were shining. "Ready to rumble, Doogal my man!" he said through his camouflage bunches. "Especially now Cherise isn't going to use up the whole lesson. Now I can really wow the crowd."

"You feel free, Dumz," I laughed. I was just hoping Miss Venter wouldn't make me speak. I don't like standing in front all alone. I'd rather do the Audience Participation part.

But that Friday, Tommy had a surprise for us too!

He grabbed Dumisani out of the line.

"Big D, listen. You know for this Free Orals lesson: Will you do something for me? Will you tell the class why I wear a balaclava? If I explain to you now, then will you explain to them?"

We Doo Dudes both stopped dead, staring at Tommy. There in the middle of the passage. Holding our breath while the rest of Grade Four SV went marching past.

Tommy gave a big sigh. "You see, my last school was in Scotland. Because my dad was on a short-term contract on the oil rigs there. And that was my sixth new school . . ."

I listened to Tommy's whole story, peering at him with one eye. When he had finished, I shook my head so I could feel the flowers swinging around on top.

"Is that all?" I demanded. "Is that the only reason? I'm telling you, Balaclava Boy, the class is going to be disappointed. Big time. They've been thinking all sorts of exciting, interesting stuff."

"I know," Tommy said. His voice was soft. "That's why I want it to stop now."

But Dumisani's eyes were shining still. "Don't worry, BB. I can still wow the crowd with this. I'll get them going. You watch. This could be good fun!"

And then we had to run. Miss Venter was waiting at the classroom door, patting her chest.

10

Friday Free Orals - Part 1

Sometimes I don't understand Dumz, even though he's my best friend in the world. Sometimes he doesn't make sense.

Like now. Why did he think Tommy's story could sound like fun? How did he think he could wow the class with it? What Tommy told us was one big letdown to me. Like opening up a huge present and finding socks inside. Or one marble. About as stupid and boring as decimal fractions.

But Dumz was bouncing around in our desk. Nearly knocking me onto the floor. Keen for Free Orals to start. He turned round to Tommy and said, "Hey, New Bru, how about this: After I explain, you come stand next to me, right? And you pull your balaclava off. Just like that! That will be a real party-time! I bet the class will enjoy that!"

Before Tommy could answer, Miss Venter was on our case. "Dumisani! Doogal! Face the front! Now, who would like to speak first?"

Dumisani's hand rocketed up. So did lots of other hands. Miss Venter chose someone from the back: someone with a pirate scarf and a nurse's hospital mask hiding her mouth and nose. Dumz and I couldn't work out who it was. We didn't recognise her voice. And we couldn't turn round to check which desk she came from.

Loudly, clearly, the girl said, "I'm going to tell you a funny story. A true funny story."

Her story was about being in a taxi called Happy Days – with a bad-tempered taxi-driver. She kept pretending to be the taxi-driver, yelling and complaining about his passengers. About the traffic. About his CD player that kept stopping and starting.

Then she pretended to be the taxi's guardtjie, saying in a squeaky voice, "Relax, my Big Boss! Chill, my Main Man. Life is good. You gotta count your blessings."

She was right. It was very funny! Around the class, everyone was falling around laughing. And then I suddenly realised who it was: Mpho, aka Mousie Mousie!

"I can't believe it, Dumz!" I whispered. "This is bizarre!"

And that's the truth. Normally Mpho says orals with

She kept pretending to be the taxi-driver, yelling
and complaining about his passengers.

her head down. Normally she speaks so softly, you can't hear a single word. Not even from the front desk.

"Must be the mask," Dumisani whispered back. He was still bouncing. His eyes were still shining.

When Mpho finished, we all cheered her back to her desk. Obakeng gave one of his steam-train whistles. Miss Venter just smiled.

The next speaker was Donna-Kyle, aka Factfile, aka Discovery Channel. We all quietened down. She often tells us interesting stuff.

She was the one who explained what 'aka' meant. Sometime early in our Grade Four year. When we were using aka all the time, trying out different nicknames for everyone.

"See," she'd told us on that Friday, "'a' is for also, 'k' stands for known and the second 'a' is for as. So when we say Kristel, aka 7de Laan, we really mean Kristel, also known as 7de Laan." And that was very interesting to know.

Today Donna-Kyle stood there in her white balaclava and said, "Do you guys know why we use the word 'balaclava'?"

"Nah!" we all shouted back.

"So shall I tell you then?"

"Yebo yes!" we shouted back. This is what Miss Venter calls Audience Participation.

So Donna-Kyle told us about a war long ago, the Crimean War, when the English and Russians were fighting. But the English soldiers were struggling because it was freezing cold and they weren't used to so much snow and ice. So the English ladies knitted them thick masks to keep their faces warm. With holes, so they could still see to shoot. And then they had a huge battle at a town called Balaclava. So the soldiers named their masks after this town.

And that was interesting too. We all clapped and cheered as Donna-Kyle sat down. Thandi and Hannah yelled, "You go, girl!"

"Dumisani? Would you like to speak next?" Miss Venter asked.

Dumisani took his time getting to the front. As he usually does for Free Orals. He took a long, deep breath and looked slowly around the classroom. Everyone was silent and still, waiting. Then he pulled his army balaclava straight. And began.

11

Friday Free Orals - Part 2

"You guys all know I don't like school much, right?" Dumisani said.

Around the class, everyone laughed. Thandi and Hannah and Innocent called out, "No lie, Big D!"

Dumisani went on. "But, dudes, I have to tell you: this week was another story. This week my mom didn't have to shout for me to get out of bed. Or into my uniform. This week Doogz didn't have to wait and wait for me outside. Hey, I couldn't get to school fast enough. Do you guys want to know why?"

"Yeah! Yeah! Yeah!" everyone chanted.

"Well, because this was the best week ever in Grade Four. The best week I've had in my whole time at school. Do you know why?"

"Why? Why? Why?" everyone chanted again. I smiled under my tea-cosy. He's the King of Audience Participation, my friend Dumz!

"Well, it's because of this new guy. And his balaclava. He made every day awesome!"

And now, with the class listening to every single word, Dumisani explained about Tommy. Just the way Tommy had explained to us. How Tommy had been to seven different schools because his dad was a short-term contractor. How Tommy had been a new pupil seven different times. And how horrible, horrible, horrible it was to be new. With everyone staring at you and whispering about you and making you feel left out and alone.

"But then, in January, he went to this new school in Scotland, right?" Dumisani went on. "And it's freezing cold there at that time. So he had to wear a balaclava. And he says it was the most amazing thing! Suddenly he didn't feel horrible. Suddenly he didn't care what the other kids did. He felt safe and comfortable and protected and not shy any more. It makes sense, right?"

Around the class, all the balaclavas and ski masks and pantyhose legs were nodding. You could feel it in the air: it made sense. Grade Four SV understood.

"So," Dumisani said, "Tommy asked Mr Rasool if he could wear one at Colliery Primary too, it being his seventh new school! Just so he wouldn't feel so bad being new. And that's the reason, dudes. That's the reason why Tommy wears a balaclava. We all guessed wrong. How about that?"

This time, everyone was quiet. Maybe they were just thinking. Or maybe they were disappointed, like I thought. But Dumisani wasn't going to leave things like that. Not in his Free Oral!

"I might have a little surprise for you," he said. "Maybe, just maybe, Tommy will take it off now. Because he's not a new boy any more. He's one of us, right?" And then Dumisani got the whole class going: "Come on, dudes! Let's hear it! Tom-mee! Tom-mee! Balaclava Boy!"

Soon everyone was chanting along: "Tom-mee! Tom-mee! Balaclava Boy!" Really enjoying themselves. I banged with my ruler on my desk to keep them all in time.

Slowly Tommy got up and went to stand next to Dumisani. He put his hands up to his balaclava and the chanting stopped. We were all dying to see what he looked like. Even if his reason wasn't so exciting.

"Just one thing," said Tommy. His voice seemed very soft and shaky. "You have to promise I can still play soccer with you. Even with my balaclava off."

Obakeng yelled from his desk, "Hey, my bru. You're our Supa Striker. Nothing's going to change that!"

Tommy nodded. And then slowly, very slowly, he began to lift his navy balaclava off his face.

I held my breath, just like before. It seemed that everyone else in Grade Four SV was holding their breath as well. Even the Dragon Lady. We watched as Tommy's face slowly appeared: his chin, his mouth, his nose, his cheeks, his forehead, his curly brown hair.

Then from all around the room came this giant gasp of amazement. All of us gasping at the same moment. We stared at Tommy, not believing our eyes. My brain felt like it was doing somersaults inside my skull. Round and round and upside down! Head over heels and back again! I reckon everyone else's brain was feeling the same way.

It was Cherise who broke the silence at last.

"This isn't Balaclava Boy, you dummies!" she said in her bossiest voice. With her pink pompom ears swinging on each side of her head. "What we have here is Balaclava Girl!"

Tommy smiled, looking embarrassed. He – she – had quite a pretty smile.

"Yes. Sorry about that. I should have told you," Tommy said. "My family calls me Tommy. But my full name is Thomasina Karen MacAdam."

And it was Dumisani, King of Audience Participation,

We watched as Tommy's face slowly appeared: his chin, his mouth, his nose, his cheeks, his forehead, his curly brown hair.

who got us all chanting again: "Thoma-Seena! Balaclava girl! Thoma-Seena! Balaclava girl!" Over and over and over.

Everyone was standing up now, enjoying the fun. So I had to get right up on top of my desk to stamp so they could keep the beat. Well, until Miss Venter asked us to please shush before Mr Rasool came to check if there was a riot in his school.

Billy de Beer, aka Lost In Space, suddenly turned away from the window, from whatever he'd been staring at all through Free Orals.

"Hey," he said in the silence, "why's the new boy got such long hair?"

And we couldn't help it, not even after what Miss Venter had just said. In one giant voice, we all yelled back:

"Because!"

THE POWERS
BY KEVIN STEVENS

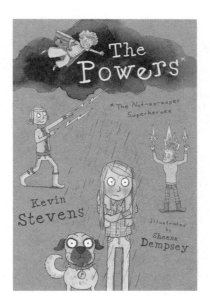

The Powers are an Irish superhero family who have some incredible powers, but seem to be seriously lacking in any ability to control them. Dad sets his head on fire, Mum brings thunderstorms everywhere she goes, JP flies into the wall more often than the sky and Suzie has had enough of the lot of them!

A perfectly-paced adventure story featuring a colourful and genuinely funny family, *The Powers* is sure to pull you into this world of disastrous heroes!

978-1-908195-83-8 / £5.99

FENNYMORE AND THE BRUMELLA
BY KIRSTEN REINHARDT

Imagine a boy living all alone in a large old house with only a sky-blue bike (who thinks he's a horse) for company. After his great-aunt dies (of dachshund poisoning – what else?) Fennymore sets off with his new friend Fizzy to find his parents and falls foul of a silvery grey gentleman and an evil doctor who wants to get his hands on a mysterious invention...

A zany adventure story with a touch of fantasy and brilliant illusrations from David Roberts.

978-1-908195-85-2 / £6.99